Eerie Elementary

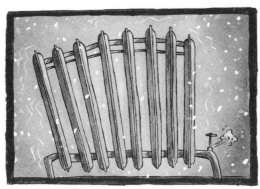

School FREEZES Over!

By Jack Chabert
Illustrated by Sam Ricks

SCHOLASTIC INC.

READ ALL THE
Eerie Elementary
ADVENTURES!

1

2

3

4

5

MORE BOOKS
COMING SOON!

TABLE OF CONTENTS

For Mum-mum. Loving you. — JC

Text copyright © 2016 by Max Brallier
Illustrations copyright © 2016 Scholastic Inc.

Chabert, Jack, author.
School freezes over! / by Jack Chabert ; illustrated by Sam Ricks.—First edition.
pages cm.— (Eerie Elementary ; 5)
Summary: A heavy snowstorm traps the students inside Eerie Elementary, a living, breathing monster brought to life by mad scientist, Orson Eerie—soon the school begins to freeze from the inside out, and Sam, Lucy and Antonio must find a way to get the heat back on before all the students freeze to death, while facing the truth that Orson Eerie is even more powerful and dangerous than they realized.
ISBN 9780545873734 (pbk. :alk. paper) — ISBN 9780545873741 (hardcover :alk.paper)
1. Elementary schools—Juvenile fiction. 2. Haunted schools—Juvenile fiction. 3. Blizzards—Juvenile fiction. 4. Best friends—Juvenile fiction. 5. Horror tales. [1. Elementary schools—Fiction. 2. Schools—Fiction. 3. Haunted places—Fiction. 4. Blizzards—Fiction. 5. Best friends—Fiction. 6. Friendship—Fiction. 7. Horror stories.
Ricks, Sam, illustrator. II. Title. III. Series: Chabert, Jack. Eerie Elementary ; 5.
PZ7.E45812 Sch 2016
813.6 —dc23 LC [Fic]
2016019784

16 15 14 13 12   20 21 22

Printed in China   62

First edition, December 2016
Illustrated by Sam Ricks
Edited by Katie Carella
Book design by Will Denton

THE STORM

"**I** can't even see outside!" Sam Graves said to his best friends, Antonio and Lucy. It was morning in Ms. Grinker's third-grade class and Sam and his friends were at their desks. A huge snowstorm was blowing outside.

"I've never seen so much snow!" Lucy said.

Antonio groaned. "I can't believe we didn't get a snow day. I should be at home on my couch!"

But Sam wasn't at all worried about the weather. He was too busy looking forward to afterschool hockey practice. Sam was terrible at most sports — but not hockey. He was one of the best skaters on the team.

Ms. Grinker and some of Sam's classmates stood at the window.

Lucy leaned across her desk and whispered, "While everyone's watching the storm, let's look at Orson Eerie's notes."

Sam nodded. "Good idea."

Orson Eerie was a mad scientist. He was also the architect who designed Eerie Elementary almost one hundred years ago. Orson Eerie found a way to live forever — he *became* the school. Orson Eerie was the school, and the school was Orson Eerie! Eerie Elementary was a living, breathing thing that fed on students.

Sam was the school hall monitor, and Lucy and Antonio were assistant hall monitors. It was their job to protect everyone. They were the only students who knew the awful truth about the school.

A few weeks earlier, the three friends had found Orson Eerie's old science book. The mad scientist hadn't wanted them to see the book. He had tried to get it back by attacking the science fair!

After defeating a giant volcano, Sam and his friends found out why Orson Eerie didn't want them reading the book: It was filled with his notes!

Sam and his friends couldn't bring the actual book to school. It was too dangerous. Instead, they took photos of the book's pages using Antonio's phone.

Antonio made sure no one was looking, and then slipped out his phone. "Orson must have written about his creepy plans in here," he whispered, as Sam and Lucy peered over his shoulder. Suddenly, he said, "Look at this! Orson wrote, 'Ways I Could Return.'"

Ways I
Could
Return:

"Return?" Lucy said. "What could that mean?"

Good question, Sam thought. *Orson already cheated death by* becoming *the school. So what could "return" mean?*

Before Sam could respond to Lucy, the wind howled. It sounded like thunder. The windows rattled and the walls shook.

WHOOOSHH! BOOM! WHAM!

The windows flew open. Thick snow blew into the classroom! The storm was now a full-on blizzard!

"Students, shut those windows!" Ms. Grinker ordered.

Sam leaned closer to his friends. "As soon as we mentioned Orson's plans to return, the storm got worse!"

"It's like Orson knows we're learning too much," said Lucy.

Students struggled to shut the windows, but the wind was too strong!

Antonio looked outside. "Do you think . . . ?"

Sam nodded. "Yes. I think Orson Eerie is controlling the weather."

WINTER WORRIES

It was chaos in the classroom. Some students kept trying to close the windows. Others ducked under their desks. Snow and ice-cold rain blew inside. All anyone could see was white, white, white. It was like the school was now at the very center of a terrible blizzard.

Noises came from the radiator in the corner. The radiator rattled and shook.

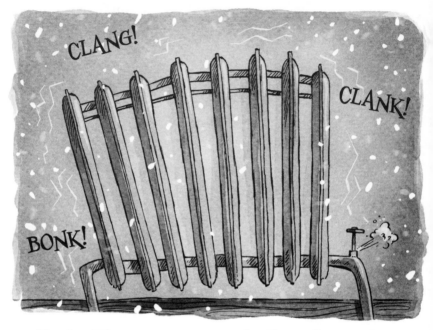

Eerie Elementary was built a long time ago. The only heat in the building came from rusty metal radiators like this one. Suddenly, there was a long, loud **HISSSSSSSS**.

The radiator shut off completely. Sam realized things had just gone from bad to worse. It felt like the temperature had dropped about twenty degrees in seconds!

Antonio eyed the thermometer on the wall. He recently did a science project on temperature, so he knew 32 degrees was when water turned to ice.

"Guys," Antonio said. "If the heat doesn't come back on soon, we'll all freeze!"

Sam's eyes darted to Antonio's phone. "What else does Orson's note say?" he asked. "The school became angry after you read it aloud, so it must be important."

The friends hurried to read more.

Sam saw the words, "A strong freeze is needed for my plan to work."

Just then, the loudspeaker squealed. The principal's voice came on. "Students, school has been cancelled —"

"Snow day!" some students cheered.

"Silence!" Ms. Grinker barked.

The principal's voice continued: "Parents have been called. Please go to your lockers and get your belongings. All classes report to the gym. Wait there until your parents arrive."

The students followed Ms. Grinker out into the hall. Sam, Antonio, and Lucy were the last to leave. Just before they stepped into the hall —

The windows suddenly slammed shut. Sam gasped. He saw ice forming around the edges. The windows were being sealed shut!

It's like the school is locking all of us inside, Sam thought.

"We need to check the front entrance!" Lucy exclaimed.

Sam and his friends raced into the hallway. They ran to the large doors that led outside.

Sam pressed his face to the window. He saw huge piles of snow forming against the door. Even worse, Sam saw ice forming on the door hinges.

"Oh no," Sam said. He pushed on the door. But it wouldn't budge.

"Let's all try at once!" Antonio said. The three friends threw their shoulders into the door. It *still* wouldn't open! "We're trapped." Sam sighed. "Trapped inside ice-cold Eerie Elementary."

ORSON'S PLAN

Sam stepped away from the door. Fear crept over him. Everyone was stuck in the school. There was no way out.

"Who *knows* how long we'll be stuck in here," Sam said. "We *need* to turn the heat back on."

Ms. Grinker shouted down the hall, "Sam, Antonio, Lucy! Hurry up and get your things!"

The three friends quickly slipped into their jackets and grabbed their backpacks.

"The binder is in my backpack," Lucy whispered.

Lucy had filled a big binder with everything they knew about Orson Eerie. It contained blueprints of the school, notes, and more.

Ms. Grinker led her bundled-up students to the gym.

Sam looked at the phone while Antonio and Lucy walked ahead.

Suddenly, Sam stopped in his tracks. His friends turned as he read words that changed *everything*: "Orson Eerie wrote, 'Once the temperature drops to 13 degrees, I will return in my human form.'"

Lucy gasped. "Do you mean . . . ?"

Sam nodded. "I think Orson was exploring ways of coming back to life — for real. Like, all the way back! A person again!"

Antonio rubbed his hands together as they continued walking. "A real, flesh-and-blood Orson Eerie?" Antonio said. "Now I've *really* got goose bumps! But I'm not sure if  they're from fear or the freezing cold . . ."

The thought of Orson Eerie returning terrified Sam. He had battled the monstrous school many times. Each fight had been awful in its own way. But Orson Eerie appearing as a real person was *horrifying*. He'd be back from the dead! He could go anywhere and do anything! He'd be more powerful than ever!

The sound of hundreds of chattering students filled Sam's ears as he walked into the gym.

"It's smart to have everyone in one room," Antonio said to his friends. "Body heat should help keep us warm."

"Hall monitors!" Ms. Grinker said as she pulled Sam and his friends aside. "Please take a quick walk around the school. Check for students who are dillydallying."

Great! Sam thought. *Ms. Grinker just gave us the perfect excuse to leave the gym!*

"You got it, Ms. Grinker!" Antonio said.

The friends rushed into the hall.

"We'll look for stragglers first," Sam said. "Then we'll get on with our real mission."

As soon as the friends were out of sight, they began running. The halls were long and winding. Sometimes, Eerie Elementary reminded Sam of a maze.

Soon, they had circled the entire school. Everyone was inside the gym.

"Okay," Sam said. "Now we need to get the heat turned back on."

"Yeah," Lucy agreed. "Before Orson comes back in human form!"

Just then, a long shadow fell over them. Sam's hair stood on end as he slowly turned around . . .

THE WET WALK

The shadow belonged to Mr. Nekobi, the old man who took care of the school.

Sam breathed a sigh of relief. "Phew!"

Mr. Nekobi was the one who had chosen Sam to be the school's hall monitor. He had told Sam, Antonio, and Lucy the truth about the school. It was a secret shared by just the four of them.

"Oh man, are we glad to see you!" Antonio said.

"We're all trapped!" Lucy exclaimed. "And Orson Eerie is behind this wild storm."

"He's trying to come back — as a real person!" Sam said.

Mr. Nekobi ran his fingers over his wrinkled chin. "I've long feared that was Orson's plan."

"We think this big freeze is part of Orson's plan to return," Sam said. "So we need to warm things up — FAST! How do we turn the heat back on?"

"The heat in this school has always been fussy," Mr. Nekobi replied.

"Just tell us what to do," Sam said.

"You'll need to go to the teachers' lounge," Mr. Nekobi said. "There, you will find a thermostat. Turn it up to the highest possible temperature. That should force the radiators back on."

"That's all?" Antonio asked. "EASY!"

Mr. Nekobi shook his head. "At Eerie Elementary, nothing is ever easy." He looked back at the gym. "I'll keep Ms. Grinker busy. Good luck . . ."

The friends took off running. But, as Sam turned the first corner, he saw that Mr. Nekobi was right. This wouldn't be easy.

The windows all flew open at once! The blizzard stormed into the hallway! Snow filled the air, and icy water splashed down.

THUMP!

SLAM!

SAA-WOOSH!

The three friends huddled together. Lucy shouted over the howling wind, "Orson's bringing the storm *inside* — to stop us!"

Slushy water flooded the hallways.

"Soon, this water will turn to ice," Sam said. "If the floors freeze, we'll *never* make it to the teachers' lounge. We'll be slipping and sliding everywhere!"

Suddenly, there was a **BZZ-ITT,** and the lights shut off. The wet hall was very dark and very spooky.

For a moment, the wind stopped wailing. A loud creaking sound filled the hall. Sam turned to see the bathroom door opening . . .

But nobody stepped through the doorway. Instead, something shiny and metal rolled out. Slushy water splashed as the strange object rolled toward them. It stopped at Antonio's feet.

Lucy gulped. The sound echoed in the quiet hallway.

Slowly, Sam crept toward the object.

"It looks like a sprinkler head," Sam said. "From the ceiling. See? It's still attached to a water hose."

CHKK-CHKK-SPiiiiTT!

Freezing cold water shot from the sprinkler head! The sprinkler leapt up! Water gushed and filled the air.

Orson Eerie had brought the sprinkler to life! It swung across the ground. Sam jumped as the hose *whooshed* beneath him.

Antonio wasn't so lucky. The sprinkler snapped out and wrapped around his ankle.

"It's got me!" Antonio shouted.

Sam and Lucy ran toward him. But they were a moment too late . . .

The hose tugged. Antonio toppled over. His cell phone slipped from his pocket and clattered to the floor.

Lighting fast, the sprinkler yanked Antonio into the bathroom. Antonio cried out. But his shrieks were cut short as the door *slammed* shut.

FROZEN!

Sam sprinted toward the bathroom door. "Come on, Lucy!" he shouted.

Lucy scooped up Antonio's phone, and ran after Sam. Together, they tugged on the knob, but the door wouldn't open.

"We're coming, Antonio!" Sam yelled through the door.

Lucy looked around, then exclaimed, "Let's grab a tool from Mr. Nekobi's supply closet! It's just down the hall."

Sam and Lucy's shoes splish-splashed as they raced down the dark, wet hallway.

Lucy yanked open the closet, and both friends rushed inside.

"A hammer!" Sam said, grabbing the tool. "This should work!"

Seconds later, they were back at the bathroom. They could hear Antonio calling for help.

"Hang on, Antonio!" Lucy shouted.

Sam banged the hammer on the doorknob.

BLAM!

BLAM!

The third time he swung, there was a loud **CRACK.** The knob broke.

Sam and Lucy pushed open the door.

With horror, they saw that Antonio's feet were frozen to the floor. The water had turned to ice! Worst of all, the sprinkler was back up in the ceiling, spraying water. Gallons of freezing-cold water rained down. It was like there was a huge rainstorm inside the bathroom.

Lucy quickly leapt up on to a chair near the door. She stuck out her hand and hoisted Sam up. Ice water pooled beneath them.

Antonio's hair and eyebrows were turning to ice!

"I-I-I can't move!" he said. His teeth were chattering. "I'm st-st-st-st-stuck!" Sam had never seen Antonio look so scared. He was shivering, and his eyes were tiny slits.

Sam knew that Eerie Elementary was a living, breathing monster. To stay alive, it must eat.

That meant . . .

"Oh no," Sam whispered to Lucy. "Eerie Elementary is turning Antonio into a Popsicle. An ice Popsicle to chomp on!"

ICICLE ALLEY

Sam and Lucy watched in horror as their friend continued to freeze. Antonio couldn't move his feet or legs. The ice held him tight.

"Don't worry, buddy!" Sam said. "We'll get you out of here."

"H-h-how?" asked Antonio.

"We'll think of something," Lucy replied.

Antonio looked his friends in the eyes. "N-n-no," he said. "Orson Eerie is trying to distract you from the real mission: getting to the teachers' lounge. So go! If you turn the heat back on, you'll stop Orson from returning. That will save everyone — even m-m-me!"

Sam's mind raced. *Yes, we need to get to the teachers' lounge. But we can't leave Antonio behind!*

Lucy said what Sam was thinking. "No way, Antonio. First, we'll get you free. Then we'll head to the teachers' lounge. It will take all three of us to defeat Orson."

Sam tried to remain calm. "So," he said, "how do we free Antonio?"

Antonio's eyes lit up. "I h-h-have an idea! My science fair p-p-project taught me that s-s-salt slows down the freezing temperature of water."

"So we need salt," Lucy said. "A lot of it!"

"I'll run to the kitchen!" Sam said.

"There could be another trap," said Lucy. "I'm going with you."

"Okay," Sam replied. "Antonio, don't worry, we won't be long!"

"You b-b-better not be!" Antonio said. If Sam and Lucy didn't hurry, he'd soon be frozen solid.

Sam set the hammer down on the sink.

An instant later, he and Lucy were both racing toward the kitchen. The temperature continued to drop. Snow swirled through the open windows, and wind whipped down the hallway. Slushy water was up to their ankles, and it was rising fast. Sam felt like they were running through a hurricane!

"Argh," Lucy groaned, as they dashed around the corner. "Nothing ruins a day like wet socks."

Sam shook his head. "That's not true. Orson Eerie ruins a day worse than *anything*." He could see his breath in the air. It was thick, like smoke.

Sam slipped. Lucy grabbed him just before he plunged into the water. Working together, they kept each other from falling.

Finally, they came to the lunchroom.

"It isn't going to be easy to reach the kitchen . . ." Lucy said, as she stood in the doorway.

The lunchroom was dark and strange shadows seemed to dance on the walls and across the wet floor. Water dripped from the sprinklers and through the ceiling tiles. Jagged icicles hung from the room's high ceiling. It was like the ceiling was covered in giant spikes!

Sam and Lucy could see the kitchen door along the far wall. But getting there seemed impossible . . .

Sam gulped. "Oh man, I wish we didn't
have to cross the lunchroom. But it's the only
way to save Antonio!"

The two friends stepped inside. Long lunch
tables filled the room.

"We'll have to run for it," Lucy said.

"Ready?" Sam asked.

Lucy nodded.

"Then let's go!" Sam shouted.

They sprinted through the lunchroom. The walls shrieked and moaned. The floors were turning to ice. Every slippery step they took seemed to make the school angrier.

They were halfway to the kitchen, when —

SMASH!

"Oh no!" Lucy yelled.

Sam eyed the spike-covered ceiling. The icicles were beginning to fall!

TURNING THE TABLES

7

Icicles crashed to the floor as Sam and Lucy raced toward the kitchen. A huge icy spike smashed right in front of them.

"Yikes!" Lucy exclaimed. "That one nearly got us!"

Sam gripped Lucy's hand. They were too far from the hall to go back. And they were too far from the kitchen to keep going.

Sam looked up. A long razor-sharp icicle hung above them. It was about to drop . . .

"Take cover!" Sam yelled.

Together, Sam and Lucy dove beneath a lunch table. A second later, there was a tremendous **CRASH!** The icicle shattered just inches from their hiding spot.

"What do we do now?" Lucy asked. "We need to get that salt before Antonio becomes an ice pop!"

They were trapped, and Sam knew time was running out.

We're safe under this table, thought Sam. *But we can't just stay here . . .*

"Wait!" Sam exclaimed. "Maybe we can bring this table with us! We'll carry it over our heads, like an umbrella — all the way to the kitchen! Like a shield!"

"That's a good idea. But look," Lucy said, pointing. The table legs were frozen solid to the floor.

Sam stared at the icy floor. *Now what?*

BREAKING FREE

T hey needed to get the table legs free from the ice. But Sam couldn't think. **SMASH! SMASH! SMASH!** Icicles crashed all around them.

Then Sam heard another sound — a sort of clanging.

"What was that noise?" Lucy asked.

"Wait a second," Sam said. "I know that sound! I hear it every day at lunch!"

Sam suddenly stuck his arm out. He reached up and felt along the tabletop.

"What are you doing?!" Lucy yelled, as an icicle slammed into the tabletop.

Then Sam's fingers felt metal. He yanked his hand back under the table. He was holding two metal lunch forks.

Lucy's eyes lit up. "Good thinking!"

Sam and Lucy quickly began jabbing the forks at the ice around the table legs.

Soon, the ice cracked. The table was free.

"Let's go!" Sam said. He and Lucy grunted as they lifted the table.

Icicles shattered against the tabletop, but it shielded them all the way to the kitchen.

At the kitchen door, they rushed out from under the table.

Sam breathed a sigh of relief. "No ice and no spikey traps in here," he said.

"Finally this school cuts us a break," Lucy said, as she grabbed a large bag of salt from the kitchen cabinet.

Sam and Lucy burst out into the hallway. They raced back to the bathroom, slipping and sliding as they ran. The two friends gasped when they entered the bathroom: Antonio was frozen up to his waist!

"What t-t-took you so long?" Antonio said.

Lucy tore open the bag of salt and poured it over the ice. Sam helped rub it in. The salt stopped new ice from forming. It was working! But it wasn't working fast enough.

"I'm going to chip away at the ice," Sam told Antonio. Sam grabbed the hammer from the sink and began banging away at the ice.

Lucy checked the thermometer. "Hurry, guys!" she yelled. "The temperature has already fallen to 19 degrees! Six more degrees, and Orson Eerie will be here — in HUMAN form!"

Sam swung the hammer one final time. Chunks of ice splintered.

"I'm free!" Antonio said, as he stepped from the crumbling ice. He huddled beneath the hand dryer. Warm air rushed over him.

Sam slipped off his jacket. "Take this, buddy," Sam said. "We can't waste any more time in this bathroom. We need to get to that main thermostat in the teachers' lounge! We need to get the heat back on. *Now!*"

HEAT RACE

Sam, Lucy, and Antonio raced toward the teachers' lounge. They were making good time. "Not much farther!" Sam called out.

As they passed the principal's office, all three friends slipped at once. The floor had become one long sheet of ice. They slid the rest of the way there.

Sam got there first. He grabbed the teachers' lounge doorknob and pulled himself up. Lucy and Antonio were close behind.

"We made it!" Sam said, smiling.

"I cannot believe we're going in here!" Antonio said. "This is like a secret world!"

They opened the door, and looked around. The teachers' lounge was dull. Nothing but newspapers and mugs and uneaten snacks.

"Well this is disappointing," Lucy said. "This is the most boring secret world ever."

But then the friends were disappointed for a different reason. They spotted the thermostat. It was trapped behind a wall of ice.

"Oh no!" Lucy exclaimed.

"Look how thick that ice is!" Antonio said.

"And it's only here . . ." Sam said, as he looked around the room. "Orson put this ice wall here, to stop us from touching the thermostat."

Antonio pounded his fists against the ice, but it was useless. And no amount of salt would help. The ice was too thick.

It would take two hundred forks and two hundred hammers to break through this, Sam thought.

They could see the thermostat through the ice. It showed the current temperature: 18 degrees, and falling fast.

"There must be another way," Antonio said. "Look through Orson's notes again. Hurry!"

Lucy quickly scrolled through Antonio's photos. Sam and Antonio peered over her shoulder. They read as fast as they could, looking for anything that might help.

Antonio shouted, "There! The page about weather experiments!"

Then Antonio read Orson Eerie's words aloud: "'My plan will work so long as no one finds the hidden switch.'"

"A hidden switch!" said Sam.

Suddenly, the walls trembled and swayed. The floor quaked.

Antonio gulped. "I think we're on the right track."

"Where could it be? We need to find that switch!" cried Sam.

"Let's check the blueprints!" Lucy said. She pulled her binder from her backpack. "I remember seeing something about a switch . . ."

She flipped through the pages.

"There!" Lucy said. She jabbed her finger at a drawing labeled SWITCH.

The friends leaned in and peered at the blueprints. At once, they exclaimed, "It's in *our* classroom!"

"Ugh! And that's all the way across the school," Antonio added. "We'll never make it in time. The hallways are solid ice!"

Sam's face lit up. He grinned as he slipped off his backpack. "I know *exactly* how we'll get there."

ON THIN ICE

Sam pulled his ice skates out of his backpack and slipped his feet inside. "It's simple! I'll skate down the hall," Sam said, "and I'll pull you guys behind me!"

"What?!" Antonio exclaimed. "How are you going to *pull* us?"

Sam whipped his orange hall monitor sash out of his backpack. "With this!"

Lucy and Antonio frowned nervously. But there was no time to argue. Sam laced up his skates. Then Lucy and Antonio tied the sash to Sam's backpack.

Lucy glanced back at the thermostat. "Only four degrees to go until Orson shows up!" she said.

"Then I'd better skate fast!" Sam said. He flung the door open.

Lucy and Antonio each stood upright behind Sam, with their sneakers flat on the ice. They gripped the sash.

"Hold on tight!" Sam yelled.

Then he skated out into the hall as hard and fast as he could, pulling them.

Sam worked up speed, and soon the three friends were zooming down the halls. Lucy and Antonio's heels skimmed along the ice's surface.

The storm blew in through the open windows. Wind howled and snow swirled around Sam as he skated. Huge snow piles had formed along the sides of the halls. Sam kept his head down, skating as fast as he could.

Antonio shouted as he glanced at the floor. "Um, Sam! Those snow piles look *alive!*"

"Antonio's right!" Lucy cried. "Watch out!"

Horrifying snow arms grew from the piles. Long, frosty fingers reached for Sam. Sam skated faster, steering into the center of the hall. Antonio and Lucy swung wildly as the monstrous hands clawed at them.

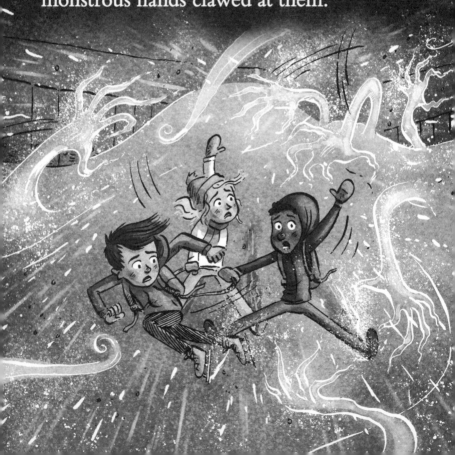

Finally, Antonio shouted, "I can see our classroom!"

"When I slow down, grab the doorway!" Sam called out.

He turned his heels and skidded to a stop.

Lucy and Antonio reached out, grabbed the door frame, and —

The three friends crashed into each other and tumbled to the floor.

But they had made it.

Together, they crawled across the ice, into their classroom: the room that held the secret switch that could stop Orson Eerie . . .

A PUZZLE TO SOLVE

Sam looked around the classroom. "Orson hid the switch somewhere in here," he said. "We just have to find it."

"We sit in here every day," Antonio said. "Wouldn't we have seen it before?"

"Think of this like a video game puzzle," Lucy said.

"Okay. But how do we *solve* it?" Antonio asked.

Outside, the wind howled. Water rained down from the sprinklers in the ceiling. The friends shivered.

Suddenly, Lucy remembered something. She pulled out the binder and started flipping pages. The ink on the pages began to run. "Look!" she said.

Lucy pointed to a photo of Orson Eerie. He was standing in their classroom almost one hundred years earlier.

"Great. A creepy old photo of Orson," Antonio said. "How does that help us?"

"Orson hid the switch when he first designed the school," Lucy explained. "So we know the switch has been here *since the beginning*. That means we need to search the room for something that hasn't changed since this photo was taken. Whatever still looks the same — that's probably where the switch is hidden!"

Orson

Eerie with Eerie's Elementary's third-grade teacher, Ms. Dempsey

SCIENCE F...
RIBBON
WINN...S

Sam nodded. If this was like a video game puzzle, then there needed to be a hint to take them to the next level. They looked at the photo, and then looked at the room.

Lucy checked the thermometer. "Hurry guys!" she said. "Only three degrees left!"

Despite the cold, Sam could feel sweat pouring off his forehead. His eyes focused on the room. Everything was different than it had been all those years ago. Different desks, different lights, different posters on the walls.

Then he saw it.

He couldn't believe it. The hiding spot had been in front of them all along!

JUST IN TIME

Sam was sure he had just solved the puzzle.

A huge smile spread across his face, and he exclaimed, "I think the switch is hidden behind the one thing we look at every day. Sometimes, like, a hundred times a day!"

Lucy's and Antonio's eyes darted to the wall. "The clock!"

Many things in the classroom had changed over the years. But the clock had not. It hung high on the wall behind Ms. Grinker's desk.

"Only two degrees left!" Lucy shouted from over by the thermometer.

Time was running out!

"I've got this one!" Antonio said, as he scrambled up on to the desk. Papers fell to the water-soaked floor.

"If Ms. Grinker saw you climbing on her desk, she'd feed you to Orson Eerie herself," said Lucy.

Antonio jumped from the desk to the bookshelf behind it. From there, he could reach the clock. He grabbed hold of it. It was ice-cold.

"Only one degree left!" Lucy announced.

"Hurry, Antonio!" yelled Sam.

The clock was stuck tight to the wall. Antonio tugged, and tugged, and tugged. Then —

The clock came free. It smashed down to the snow-covered floor. Leaning forward, Antonio peeked through the hole that clock had kept hidden.

"I see a metal switch!" Antonio said.

"Pull it!" Sam shouted. "We're almost out of time!"

Antonio reached in and pulled the switch.

Nothing happened.

Lucy looked around. "Um, why isn't anything —"

HISSSS!!!!!

The radiator shrieked. The walls rumbled. Heat began to flood the room.

"We did it! The heat is back on!" Sam exclaimed.

"It already feels warmer!" Lucy said.

Antonio jumped down from the desk. "We stopped Orson Eerie from coming back!"

The three friends were about to high-five when they heard a loud **BANG.** Sam teetered toward the door. He looked out into the hallway, just in time to see the front doors fly open.

A dark cloud of snow and rain and hail came spinning into the hall!

Sam saw that this storm was different.

He gasped. "It's Orson Eerie," he said. "He's an icy, monstrous *tornado!*"

A WALL OF WINTER

The tornado was spinning and swirling down the hall. Sam wanted to just let the icy storm pass. But he knew Orson Eerie fed on students. And he knew if Orson Eerie made it to the gym, he would feast on everyone!

"We need to destroy the tornado!" Sam shouted over the wind.

"How?" Antonio asked.

"This isn't a regular tornado," Sam replied. "It's made of ice and snow. So we should be able to beat it with . . ."

"Heat!" Lucy exclaimed.

"So where's the hottest place in school?" asked Antonio.

Lucy began flipping through the blueprints. "The big radiator outside the gym!" she said.

"Then that's where we're going!" Sam said.

He looked down at the floor. The heat had caused a thin layer of water to form, but the ice was still thick enough for skating. "Hold on tight!"

Lucy and Antonio grabbed on to the sash, and Sam skated out into the hallway. He took off, towing his friends behind him.

SCREECH! The tornado made a sound like nails on a chalkboard.

Swirling mist filled the hallway. Hail pounded the lockers. Water splashed the friends' backs. Furious winds pulled at them. Their jackets whipped about.

Sam glanced over his shoulder as he skated. Just behind his friends, he saw the speeding tornado. It was gaining on them . . .

Sam's heart was pounding. Sweat dripped down his back. His legs felt weak. He still had two long hallways to skate before he reached the radiator.

"I can't skate fast enough!" Sam called to his friends. "Orson's catching up to us!"

For a moment, all Sam heard was the roaring tornado.

Then Lucy said something *crazy*: "Antonio and I will let go!"

"What?!" cried Antonio. "That tornado will suck us right up!"

"Sam will be able to skate to the radiator without us slowing him down," explained Lucy. "It's the only way we'll stop Orson!"

Antonio's voice was firm. "Okay," he said.

Before Sam could say "no," they let go of the sash!

He looked back. It was like watching a movie in slow motion. Sam saw Antonio's and Lucy's eyes go wide as they were lifted off their feet. They were yanked into the air and pulled into the dark, spinning cloud.

Sam looked away. He couldn't believe what Lucy and Antonio had just done. Now more than ever, he *had* to reach the radiator. He had to get there. It was the only way to save his friends!

Sam lowered his head. Without the extra weight of Lucy and Antonio, he was skating much faster.

The Orson Eerie storm changed one last time as it sped toward Sam. It took the form of a wicked snow monster! The bottom was only swirling ice and snow.

Horror filled Sam as he saw that it had a body and a face.

It was clearly Orson Eerie. Sam and his friends had stopped Orson Eerie from taking *human* form, but this was still very close — and still very scary.

Sam saw flashes of his friends. They twirled helplessly in the swirling icy air below the floating face.

Sam knew the monster would chase him. And he knew he needed to lead the monster to the radiator. Or else his classmates and his teachers — *everyone* inside the school — would be doomed!

He didn't have much time!

SOME LIKE IT HOT

Sam skated faster and faster. The horrible snow monster was right on his heels.

Sam spotted the radiator. It loomed ahead of him. It was huge — taller than he was, and it was old and rusty. He zoomed toward it!

He turned his heels and slid to a sharp hockey stop. Ice sprayed the radiator, and the rusty metal sizzled.

Sam's mind raced as the storm bore down on him. *I need to wait until the last moment to get out of the way,* he thought. *I need to trick this icy monster into slamming into the radiator. It's the only way to defeat the spinning tornado and release Lucy and Antonio!*

The radiator hissed and rumbled. Sam felt like his back was on fire. But he didn't move.

The monstrous snowman swirled and spun toward him.

Sam waited.

Its eyes stared at him.

But still, Sam waited.

Lucy and Antonio swirled in the air, spinning around and around.

But still, Sam held his ground.

The storm's face grinned at Sam — a grin full of icy fangs! The terrible storm was almost upon him.

Then, at the very last second, Sam dove! He hit the floor beside the radiator with a loud **WHOMP.** He felt the ice and snow whoosh past him.

A second later —

KA-BOOM!!!

The horrible snow monster slammed into the radiator! The radiator cracked open from the force. Hot steam burst forth and mixed with the ice and snow. A misty cloud filled the hallway. It was so thick that Sam could barely see anything.

Then —

PLOP!

THUMP!

Lucy and Antonio crashed to the floor beside Sam.

The mist began to disappear. Then a sound came from deep within the school . . .

AAAARGGH!

Sam knew it was the pained howling of Orson Eerie. Sam knew he had put a stop to Orson's evil plan.

SNOW DAY

The sound of opening doors filled the school. Defeating Orson Eerie caused the snowbanks and the ice to melt — instantly! The students were no longer trapped.

Parents rushed into the school.

Lucy and Antonio sat up. They both looked dazed.

"Are you guys okay?!" Sam asked.

"Ooof," Antonio groaned. "I feel like I just rode the Tilt-A-Whirl nine times in a row."

"I think I'm okay . . ." Lucy said. "We did it, didn't we?"

Sam grinned. "We did."

Just then, Ms. Grinker marched over.

Sam gulped.

"You three!" she barked. "What are you doing out here? And Sam, are you wearing your *ice skates* inside school?"

"Um, well," Sam stumbled. "I have hockey practice today."

"I think you got plenty of practice already, buddy," Antonio joked.

Mr. Nekobi walked out into the hallway. "Ms. Grinker," he said, interrupting her. "Were any other students missing from the gym today?"

Ms. Grinker thought for a moment. "Well, no . . ."

"Then I think our hall monitors did a wonderful job," Mr. Nekobi said, steering her toward the gym.

Sam untied his skates and slipped back into his sneakers.

Then, Sam, Lucy, and Antonio headed toward the exit. Students and parents hurried past them. But the three best friends took their time. They were tired and did not want to do any more racing around.

They spotted their parents outside. But before they walked over, Lucy stopped. "Guys," she said, "There's something I have to tell you. When I was inside that tornado, I felt something . . . I *felt* Orson Eerie."

Antonio nodded. "I felt it, too. He's even more dangerous and powerful than we ever thought . . ."

Lucy's words made Sam's skin crawl. It took a moment before he could speak again. "We *must* stop him," Sam finally said. "We thought Orson Eerie had one goal: swallow students to stay alive. But now we know that was only part of his plan. His *real* goal is to come back to life."

Lucy nodded. "And who knows how many other ways he might be able to do that. This freeze plan was probably just one of many!"

"I bet Orson's old science book holds more clues," Antonio added.

Sam shoved his hands into his pockets. The air was chilly, and his clothes were still damp. "Well," he said, "it sounds like we've got a *lot* of studying to do to protect the students of Eerie Elementary."

Shhhh!

This news is top secret:

Jack Chabert is a pen name for Max Brallier. (Max uses a made-up name instead of his real name so Orson Eerie won't come after him, too!)

Max was once a hall monitor at Joshua Eaton Elementary School in Reading, MA. But today, Max lives in a weird, old apartment building in New York City. His days are spent writing, playing video games, and reading comic books. And at night, he walks the halls, always prepared for the moment when his building will come alive.

Max is the author of more than twenty books for children, including the middle-grade series The Last Kids on Earth and Galactic Hot Dogs.

Sam Ricks went to a haunted elementary school, but he never got to be the hall monitor. As far as Sam knows, the school never tried to eat him. Sam graduated from The University of Baltimore with a master's degree in design. During the day, he illustrates from the comfort of his non-carnivorous home. And at night, he reads strange tales to his four children.

How much do you know about
Eerie Elementary
School FREEZES Over?

What happens to make Sam think Orson Eerie is behind the snowstorm?

Why was it hard to turn the heat back on?

Why did Lucy and Antonio let the tornado suck them up?

Look back at page 82. What is Sam's plan to defeat Orson Eerie?

What is Orson Eerie's real goal? Write a story and draw pictures to show what **you** think Orson might try next to reach this goal.